Bold and the Magic Stove

By David J M Russell

To Joe

Jam David.

The following story is entirely fictional. Any resemblances to real people, living or dead, is purely coincidental.

Artwork by Purevsuren Lhavgasuren

and David J M Russell

Bold and the Magic Stove

ACKNOWLEDGMENTS

Thanks to my wife, Doljin, and my children Billy, Misheel and Maral for inspiring me to write this book.

I would also like to thank the many people who helped get this book out and about notably the online community for their technical and marketing experience, two things I have little experience in.

Chapter 1 – The Beginning

It was yet another dusty day in the Gobi desert. There was nothing much to see outside here apart from endless rocks and stones and the occasional pile of sand. It was a dry, dusty empty place with few people. In winter it was freezing and in summer it was very, very hot. Little Bold loved it but at the age of 3, he had not seen anything else. He did not know what a tree or a forest was. Or a farm. Or a river. Or even a city. All he knew was this desert. This was little Bold's world and his parents and older sister Sara were well aware of this fact. As soon as the yurt door was opened, including at dawn, he would charge towards the outside world – even if it was bitterly cold or scorching hot outside. Everyone who met Bold, even at this young age, saw he had so much energy for such a young child, so much curiosity in the world around him. They knew life would have a lot to offer Bold in the future.

The Old man sat in front of his stove drinking milk tea, like he had always done. He looked at the stove, which was a normal Mongolian stove. It was just like any other stove that people had in their yurts. It was circular with a grill at the front, a round removable plate on top and a chimney going up through centre of the yurt. There was, however, one unusual thing about the stove – it had a small circular blue light on the front. Slightly raised up from the metal, it was possible to press it in and out but nothing seemed to happen. Nobody really knew how it worked. Sometimes the light was on, sometimes it was off. All the old man knew was that the stove had changed his live forever. From the day he received it and took it home all those years ago, his live would become one long chain of adventures, all linked together by one thing: the old stove. The magical stove. He looked at it again and smiled. Who knows? Maybe the stove was looking back. He had often asked himself that question.

The old man often wondered about the future. When he died what would happen to the stove? Which one of his children would have it, or would even want it? He slowly rose from his bed and poured more tea. The door opened and some people came in. An older girl quietly entered the yurt, but leading the way was a young boy, about 3 years old. He was quick. He ran over to the old man and launched himself into his arms. That was young Bold and the old man his uncle. His strange old uncle with all his tales that nobody ever believed. Weird and wonderful things that were obviously impossible; goats made of sand and fake mirages full of sweet fermented horse milk. Orange groves sprouting from horse dung. Bold liked the old man and he liked going to his yurt. But he particularly liked his stove – the special one that had that little blue light at the front which nobody was allowed to press. However, being a 3 year old boy wanting to discover the world around him, he went ahead and pressed it anyway. In fact, he would do it every time he visited his uncle. Bold had few other memories of his uncle, his yurt or the stove after those early days.

Chapter 2 – Under the Tunnel

Bold was now a big boy and no longer a 3 year old child, but a 4th grade elementary student, aged 10. His sister Sara was 18 and had just started studying at the local agricultural college. It was spring and many students and other people were outside cleaning the drainage ditches. It was a horrible job but somebody needed to do it. The day was nearly finished and everybody was tired and hungry.

'Come on Bold. Let's go home,' shouted Sara as she grabbed her bag. Bold was still in the ditch, not cleaning up but looking for stuff that might be of interest to a ten year old boy. He picked up a broken spade. 'Nahhh. Useless,' he said to himself. Then he picked up an old plastic box and tossed it back. Then he saw the tunnel. It had already been partly cleaned out but there was a lot of potentially interesting junk still there. So he headed over to have one last look before his sister started getting angry.

The stove was half hidden under some discarded plastic bags and a box of animal bones, plastic bottles and old cans. Nothing interesting.

Then Bold noticed it. He stopped abruptly and leaned forward to get a better view. He was now in the tunnel and in the darkness and his eyes had not adjusted yet. He leaned forward a little more and squinted his eyes. Gradually the silhouette of the old stove materialized in front of him.

'Fantastic!' he said out loud to himself.

'Hurry up you,' shouted his sister, 'I'm hungry.'

'Wait, I've found something.'

'Well, leave it. Let's go.'

'No. Give me a hand. It's heavy. Bring your friend. Is Jargal still there?'

She looked at Jargal, 'no she…,' she was about to say that her friend had already left.

'I'll help you,' said Jargal, obviously not wanting to go.

'Come on Sara,' and dragged her reluctant and tired friend down into the murky tunnel. *This better be worth it*, thought Sara as she followed her friend.

It didn't take long for them to get back to their third floor flat. The stove wasn't too heavy and they got some men to help lifting it up the stairs and a guy with a pick-up truck also helped them — for a fee of course. The biggest problem was going to be trying to explain it to his mum. They had to clean it and put it on the balcony amongst all the other random broken bits and pieces which seemed to end up out there. And then there were all the various boxes and jars and bottles which people in his family seemed to collect but never use.

He still didn't really know why he brought it back but he remembers some old man from his childhood having one just like it and he had seen other people in yurts using them. At least, that is what he thought — how was he to know that his Uncle's stove had been abandoned long ago and had ended up in a tunnel along a drainage ditch, under a road not so far from where he lived? Of course, it WAS his uncle's old stove. It would be a while before Bold would realize this though. But he was happy with what he had found—no matter who its previous owner was.

Chapter 3 Weird Taps

It all started just after breakfast on Monday morning. Sara opened the door to the balcony. It was nice and bright outside. A perfectly cool Mongolian spring morning; dry fresh snow lying on the ground. She looked down and watched a group of kids playing as they went to school, a young college boy obviously in a rush somewhere and the familiar early morning calls of the milk and cheese sellers. She casually discarded the plastic bag full of old bottles and jars. Some fell out onto the balcony floor but Sara was in too much of a rush to tidy up.

Then something strange happened: an empty carton of apple juice and then an empty bottle of soy sauce tumbled out the top of a plastic bag full of trash and scraped past the blue light on the stove and, just for an instant, they both touched the outer glass cover. Silence and no movement. And then, magically the little blue glass light on the front of the stove began to glow blue – as if it were some sort of machine warming up; very dull and distant at first but soon it became a full but small piercing blue light. But still silent and still.

'Bold. Quickly! You need to have a shower this morning. There was no water yesterday. Oh, *is* there any hot water?' His mum shouted, 'I need to go now. Remember and lock the door. Bye.' Bold was only half listening as he closed the bathroom door. Still half asleep and looking not unlike a zombie, he leaned forward and turned on the taps.

Splutter. Splat. The taps started spitting at him like they usually do when there is no water available.

Hmm he thought. No water again. He waited one minute – nothing. Two minutes - nothing. Then.....Wait. What was that? Very faint sounds. Getting louder. Getting louder.

At last, water. It's coming. And then a few drips. Funny smell. Not copper this time, as is often the case. Then the water came gushing out. Not clear. Not murky yellow like what usually happens when the pipes are flushing out but a sort of 'greeny' colour and.......what is that smell.......apple? APPLE? Apple juice was coming out the taps. Apple Juice.

Bold jumped back in surprise and in disbelief. The bath was beginning to fill-up. Both taps. Hot

10

and cold apple juice. Would he get in? Well, he WAS a bit dirty……

So in he went and started washing in apple juice. Splashing and laughing, Splashing and laughing and making a right old mess.

'I am having an apple juice bath. Brilliant! Wait until I tell my friends.'

He was ecstatic and wanted to get to school as quickly as he could. As soon as he finished, he jumped out the bath, quickly dried himself and put on his school uniform, rushed out the house (remembering to lock it) and ran all the way to school.

Fifteen minutes later the teacher walked into class.

'Sit down children. Books out. *Sit down* I said Deggi. You too Amra.' She slightly sniffed the air. *Smells funny in here,* she thought.

Five minutes later: 'Is someone eating in class? You know the rules. No eating in class.' Nobody was eating.

'Somebody is eating in class,' the teacher said 'I smell...*sniff sniff*...apples.'

The kids looked around looking for the apple-eating criminal. Nobody was guilty.

'It's me,' said Bold, 'but I wasn't eating apples.' *Eh!!!!!!* thought everybody else in the class.

'I had an apple juice bath this morning.' He was so happy and wanted to tell the world about his magic taps that flowed apple juice. Hot and cold apple juice.

'What?! Don't be smart Bold. Very funny. Ha

Ha.' His teacher said, being sarcastic.

'No. it's true. My bath has apple juice.'

His classmates looked at each in disbelief. *What is he doing? Does he want to die by the hands of The Dragon Teacher? What was that boy thinking of?*

'Do you think I am stupid?' his teacher demanded, followed by nervous laughs from the class which irritated The Dragon Teacher even more.

'Honestly, I am not lying.' he insisted.

That was enough. She had had enough and promptly marched Bold to the principal's office. He didn't believe him either. Nobody did of course. Apple juice from taps? Nonsense.

Lunchtime. So Bold went home. All his friends at school were laughing at him and his teachers were disappointed at his lies.

On his way home, some older boys (Dorj and Baatar) saw him and started laughing and shouting at him.

'Apple juice baths! You are stupid Bold. Crazy!' and they started to throw snow and dirt at him and started to play wrestle, pulling him onto the ground like wrestlers do. His clothes got all dirty. Then the boys got bored and just left him, but Bold wasn't too bothered. They were stupid boys anyway and Bold knew he was smarter. He knew their names also but had his own names for them – They were always together so he simply referred to them as The Idiots. He never said those names in front of them though. They were a little too big for him. Anyway, soon after they left, he met his mum outside their home.

'Look at you!' she said 'What happened? You are so dirty. Did you fall? Were you fighting again?'

'No....I..'

'Well go home and have a shower again. Get cleaned up. If your dad comes home and finds out you have been fighting, you will be in trouble. Big trouble.'

'But I haven't been fighting,' but his mum wasn't listening to him. So he went home and got ready to have a shower. *No more apple juice* he thought to himself, already wanting to forget the morning's events.

Five minutes later he was standing in the bathroom again. And again there was no water. Then the same thing happened again. Clanking noises. Hissing. No water. Then it came. Water. Hot and cold. Loads of it. No! Bold wasn't going to settle for a shower – he wanted a bath – a long deep bath to get rid of the dirt but also to get rid of the apple juice smell. The apple juice shower that seemed to be so great at first but, in the end, had given him too many problems. The kids thought he was crazy, his teachers thought he was a troublemaker. But he knew he was neither. So he lay down in the warm bath and just relaxed. Big deep breath. AAhhhh....... He was completely relaxed.

The problem was it wasn't water. Nor was it apple juice. It was.....soy sauce. Dark, rich soy sauce. But to Bold, it was water. He couldn't see it or smell it. But - it wasn't exactly soy sauce either. It looked like water. It smelt like water but.....well....something *had* happened the night before and changed water into apple juice. Was it going to happen again? Happen for the second day running. As everybody was sleeping, would that blue light come on again?

The morning started like any other morning – Bold and Sara went to school and college, their mum took Zolboo to his grandmothers, their dad was still away working. Bold went to school and a few of the kids mocked him again but Bold didn't care. He got his work done and he was friends again with the teachers. The day was normal; the blue light hadn't come back on. Yesterday's weird events were already beginning to look like a dream and Bold was very, very relieved......BUT....wait a minute! Everything was not as normal as it seemed.....

(Back at home, all was silent in the house. All was silent on the balcony. The stove stood there silent and motionless. But something was beginning to happen. Again. At first a faint dull glow but gradually that blue light on the stove started to shine again.)

The school day was coming to an end and it was time to tidy up the classrooms.

'Bold. Can you go and get the broom from room 14 please,' asked his teacher.

'Ok.' So off he went to get the broom.

Room 14 was empty. He got the broom and headed back to his classroom. He opened the door and..............silence. Then The Dragon Teacher turned to look at Bold and got such a fright her glasses fell off.

'AHHH!!!' she screamed. The children didn't know whether to laugh or run away or cry.

It was very, very funny but that boy Bold looked very, very scary. Bold was completely covered in dark soy sauce. His hair and clothes and skin were all dark brown, sticky and smelly. And he smelt something awful. *What is going on?* Bold thought, having no idea what he looked or smelt like.

18

'Who are you?' demanded the teacher, not recognizing him. 'What do you want? Is that my broom? Where is Bold? What have you done with Bold?'

'Ehh. I am Bold. It's me. What are you talking about? Here's the broom. For the floor, you sent me to get the broom. Here it is. What's the problem?'

'My goodness, it *is* you,' she said leaning forward squinting her spectacle-less eyes, 'you are all... brown and you smell like....I don't know.... Your hair. Your face. Your clothes. You are covered in.. *thinking, sniffing*....Soy Sauce.'

'What?'

He thought the teacher had gone mad. Bold wasn't even sure he knew what soy sauce was. But all the kids were looking at him as if he had just come from another planet and the kids closest to him were also holding their noses. Then some slowly started to giggle nervously. The teacher put her classes back on.

'What did you do?' She asked him. Bold was still completely baffled by the teacher and the kids' reactions. Of course, he couldn't smell or see any

19

soy sauce. But everybody else could.

'I went to get your broom, like you asked,' was Bold's honest but insufficiently convincing reply which, naturally, was not enough to prevent him getting into deeper trouble. Now the nervous giggling erupted into wild laughter – which made his teacher even angrier, of course. Bold didn't really know what to think or do, but he had to get out the classroom somehow. So he quietly slipped away and headed home, leaving his crazy teacher pulling her hair out and his classmates rolling around the floor in laughter.

Bold was in deep trouble. Nobody believed him. And he didn't want to speak to anybody. He was, truly, in a huff. He arrived home and this time he didn't want to have a shower. He just wanted to lie down and have a sleep, so he lay down on the sofa and closed his eyes. He was soon asleep. About twenty minutes passed when he heard the keys at the door. His mum was home.

'AHHHH', she screamed 'Who are you? What are you doing in my house?' she said on seeing Bold lying on the sofa.

He immediately jumped up from the sofa.

'It's me, mum.'

'Eh...! What's that on your face and clothes? What have you been doing? What's that stink? Go and change and wash immediately. Wait until I tell your father when he returns. You are in big trouble.'

So Bold was, yet again, in the bad books. And he still had no idea what everybody was going on about soy sauce for - and still nobody believed his apple juice story. *World—just leave me alone.*

Out on the balcony, the empty bottle of soy sauce and the empty cartoon of apple juice lay still on the balcony floor. Next to them the blue light on the stove faded away. No movement. No sound and no light. Normality returned to the balcony and the world beyond.

That night it was snowing again. It was also a little windy. On the balcony, Bold's orange plastic sledge stood upright against the railing. It started moving as the wind pushed it. Then the wind got stronger. It moved again. Then it fell and on the way bashed into the little blue light on the stove. Then the light came slowly back on.

Chapter 4 – Gone sledging

Bold woke up before anyone else. It was Saturday morning. Sara also had a day-off from college- she was still sound asleep. Bold lay in bed and thought about the previous day - apple juice and soy sauce. He hoped that all the strange happening would be forgotten and it would just be a normal day- like any other. So he got up, checked his little mobile phone, 0745 the clock said. Then he turned on the TV and watched a bit of Cartoon Network. Sid Mental was on – his favourite. An hour later, everybody was up.

'Let's go sledging,' shouted Bold, to nobody in particular, as he opened the curtains and saw the fresh new snow. Sara thought about it for a moment and agreed. It looked great outside. And at this time of year new snow doesn't often stay for long; tomorrow it could be t-shirt weather – again. Make the most of it. Their mother would stay at home and look after Zolboo and Bold and Sara would go sledging. Bold would phone his friend Amra to see if he wanted to go.

'I'll get the sledge,' he shouted, again to nobody in particular. So he opened the balcony door, shuffled past all the stuff and pulled up his sledge, bringing it into the kitchen. Him and Sara got ready and in a short time were ready to leave the house.

The best place for sledging was Buman Hill, a few kilometers out of town. It was a bit of a trek across the fields and up the hill but, because of the further distance, was usually quieter. There were two other closer places but the slopes weren't as long or steep and most people went there because they were more accessible for people without cars or without 4WD vehicles. It was still early in the day so the extra trek would be worth it.

Bold was already struggling. They were only about 100 metres from their apartment building, but off the road and heading away from town.

'Hey! Wait up,' said Bold to Amra and Sara. She was quicker and older; he didn't have a sledge to pull.

'It was your idea to go to Buman Hill. You still want to go?' shouted Sara.

'Yes. It is much better. But just slow down.'

'Ok. We will,' shouted Amra as he pushed Sara

to the ground, turned and started running up the hill.

Bold just sighed. 'We have all day, why the rush?' So he sat down for a rest. The ground was beginning to slope upwards but he still wasn't really at the bottom of the hill yet. He would be there soon. A little rest and some snacks would give him the energy for the final push. He looked up the hill and saw his friend and sister still running. THEY were already half way up the hill.

'I'll catch up, later,' he said loudly as he opened a Mars and drank some bazooka-ade. He plonked himself down on the sledge and ate his snacks. He had about another 100-150 metres to go before the bottom of the hill, then a few more up to the top. Not that much, but tough going as the snow was getting deeper as he went. There were a bunch of pine trees at the top where he could hang his bag and coat if it got warmer. There might also be some people there later in the day, but at this time, it would probably be deserted. He sat there quite content and was about to get up and head up the slope after the other two when he thought he sensed the sledge moving. He paused and shuffled around a bit knowing that it was just his imagination. Maybe the sledge slipped off a stone or something. Who knows? It was nothing anyway.

Then a sudden short jerk.

Bold shot to his feet as quickly as if something had tried to bite a chunk out his bottom.

'What was that...!' he shouted rather loudly. Up the hill Amra stopped, turned round and looked down towards Bold. Had he heard anything? The sledge was still. It hadn't moved. It was just his imagination.

Just my imagination thought Bold.

Nevertheless, he looked around as if checking that people weren't watching him. He was a tad embarrassed although nobody was there. He felt a bit stupid. He looked at the sledge again. Had it moved? He thought not. He stood and looked at it. Seemed like for ages. Was he going to sit on it again? Well he had too. So he carefully lowered himself onto it. Nothing happened, of course.

Then it suddenly jerked forward again. Bold sat upright. Not again. Bold was sure it was not his imagination. Then it jerked forward again, but this time it didn't stop. It slowly continued to move forward...and ...eh...*upwards*? Bold noticed it was moving *upwards*. Then it got faster. Bold tightened his grip on the sledge's sides.

'Oh no, this cannot be happening. No way.' He closed his eyes and opened them to make sure everything was real. It was and the sledge was getting faster. And faster. Maybe jogging pace. And faster. Running pace. He was also beginning to smile and lose his fear of the weirdness.

Hey, actually, this was brilliant. Faster.

'Weh hay!' he shouted to nobody in particular. 'I am going uphill on a sledge. No hands'.

Then the sledge suddenly darted off to the right and ran almost at right angles to its original route. It wasn't going up the hill – it was going around the hill, heading towards the trees.

'Oh no!' shouted Bold as the sledge flew past a stump, bypassed a fallen trunk and missed a few dozen trees by the odd centimetre or two. Out of the trees and back onto the grass and again the sledge changed direction and powered on up the hill, Bold holding onto the sides like a maniac with a BIG grin on his face, trying not to laugh too loudly. Then the sledge slowed down and Bold soon realized he was at the top of the hill. *Wow. Look at this*, he thought.

The hill looked great. The snow was fresh with no human (or animal tracks). He was the first. Then he remembered his sister and Amra....

He could hear them further down the hill, Sara pulling the sledge; Amra running on a little ahead. They were about 300-400 metres away, down the slope. He laughed. But then a rather worrying thought came into his head. How was he going to explain how he got up to the top so quickly? They would never believe him if he told them about his sledge going uphill on its own. Think of something.

Quickly.

A tractor? *A farmer gave me a lift in his tractor*. No.

A jeep passed and gave me a lift. No, these wouldn't do. Where are the tracks?

A horse. *A guy on a horse gave me a ride*? No. Again no tracks.

Ehhh.....

Helicopter....?

A UFO....?

A....No, this was getting silly now. He would have to think of something. They were getting closer. Too late....! He was spotted. He could see them both looking up the hill, both standing there still. He was sure they couldn't believe what they were seeing.

'Is that you?' Amra shouted.

Bold froze. What was he going to say? *Brilliant* he thought as some idea lodged itself in his head.

'Yes. Of course! Who do you think it is? Hurry up....'

Now the masterstroke of pure genius –

'I've been waiting here for ages. Thought you'd never get here. What's the problem down there?'

They were baffled to say the least. Amra turned to Sara, 'How come he's up there? Did he pass us? Can you see any tracks?' Of course, Sara couldn't answer these questions. She just shrugged.

'I really have no idea how he got up there so quickly. He must have got a lift. Let's get up there anyway. I'm sure we will find out when we get to the top.'

'What next?' thought Bold aloud. What was he going to tell them once they were up? He had an idea. He was just going to ignore everything and act as if nothing had happened and give as normal and logical an answer to any questions they might ask....which he thought might be many.

It wasn't long before they were up at the top beside Bold. Amra bent over and put his hands on his knees; Sara looked less tired. She didn't say anything as she walked over to Bold who was sitting on his sledge eating some crisps. She was looking around trying to find clues to how he got up there. No tracks – car or any other kind. Then she saw the marks the sledge made in the snow.

'You came from over THERE?' she sort of asked Bold and asked herself at the same time. Bold looked over to the sledge marks and simply nodded.

'How?'

'I just came up that way,' he replied very matter-of-fact and without saying too much.

'You get a lift?'

'No'

'You walked?'

'I came up that way,' he repeated waving his arm casually in the direction of the tracks. Then he noticed something he hadn't thought about. There were sledge tracks alright but no footprints. So he couldn't say he had simply found a shortcut and walked. They would know he wasn't telling them the truth.

Meanwhile Amra had recovered and had come over to join them. He had been listening but hadn't said anything yet.

'You came that way?' he asked, looking down at the footprint-less sledge tracks.

'Yip,' Bold said.

'On the sledge?' *Oh no,* thought Bold. *You've been rumbled.* There was a pause. Seemed to last forever.

'Fair enough,' he said turning round and taking a big chunk out of his apple.

What a Dummy!

Bold had got away with it. *Had they simply accepted his answers*? Sara wasn't convinced though.

'You just ran up there pulling your sledge?' she asked. 'Must be very tired. Must have eaten a lot of bananas and chocolate. All that energy. Huh,' she added with a hint of sarcasm. Bold sensed she didn't believe him but played along. He just smiled and said nothing.

'Weird though....' she continued then paused. She started walking faster in front of Bold then playfully but deliberately she turned and smiled at him, '....No footprints...' she said very matter-of-fact.

Nuclear explosion in Bold's head. He waited for the fallout. But........nothing. She said nothing. He felt guilty, for sure, but also mightily relieved.

Sara then jumped on Amra's sledge. 'Come on Amra,' she yelled, 'get on.' He obliged and they were soon careering down the slope. 'Last one down is a fat horse,' Amra shouted.

Bold didn't take up the challenge. He sat on his sledge feeling incredibly relieved. He had got away with it after all. They need never know that his sledge went up the hill on its own. He thought about that for a moment. That's impossible, isn't it?

The Idiots, Baatar and Dorj approached him from behind. They were waiting for their moment. The other two were gone now and Bold was on his own. But Bold got up and pulled his sledge over to a better slope. He was going down after Amra and his sister. They had better make their move.

'Oi!' shouted Baatar. Bold turned round. *Oh no.* he thought as he saw The Two Idiots. *What were they doing up here?*

'What you doing here?' he asked, pretending he was already bored by their presence but actually a bit worried.

'We are here to sledge....and break yours.' At that, Dorj revealed a large stone he had hidden under his coat. He lifted it up and.....

..*CRASH!*

It came crashing down on Bold's sledge, breaking it completely in two with lots of sharp plastic splinters in the snow. They both looked at Bold, waiting for some kind of reaction, then simply turned and headed back the way they had come, taunting and laughing at Bold as they went. Bold was in shock. Not angry, not upset, just numb. He had a long walk back down. He stayed there for about 5 minutes – alone in the silence and cold – it was getting colder. He sat down and checked if he had any food left in his bag. He didn't know what to do with his sledge. Then it happened.

At first, all he heard were a few scraping and shuffling noises on the snow; like some small rodents scurrying beneath the surface. But there were no rodents. Even after being taken for an impossible uphill ride on his sledge, he still couldn't believe what he was seeing. The broken bits of the sledge were.......coming back together. The sledge was repairing itself! The broken parts were bonding and the cracks were sealing themselves. In less than a minute the sledge was completely fixed. He rubbed his eyes. That didn't work. The sledge was definitely *not* broken. He cautiously picked it up and turned it over. Examining up close the parts of the sledge which had been shattered or cracked, he still couldn't believe what he was seeing.

But not only was it fixed, it was actually better than before, looking somewhat shinier. All the scrapes and scratches it had from previous sledging adventures had completely disappeared. It was perfect, better than brand new.

Carefully he put the sledge on the snow, aiming it down the slope. Slowly and purposely, he lowered himself into position (just in case the cracks opened up again). All was fine. He pushed gently forward with his two arms and slowly the sledge gathered pace. In no time, he was whizzing down the slope. *Blimey*, he thought, *it is going much faster than before.* And so it was – it was going like a bullet, like a bobsleigh, like some kind of souped-up, turbo-charged power sledge. It wasn't long before he saw some figures ahead – Amra and Sara, he thought. But wait, there were more. There were four people at the bottom of the slope – they had been joined by The Idiots.

They were quick Bold thought out loud. In fact, they had headed down the slope soon as they had wrecked Bold's sledge, almost going the same route Bolds magic sledge had taken him on his route to the top. Bold gradually came to a halt about 10 metres from where Sara, Amra and The Idiots were standing.

'What kept you?' Amra asked.

'My sledge. I had a problem with it. Seems fine now,' he said, pretending to ignore the Idiots but secretly looking for their reaction.

'Problem? What kind of problem can you get with a sledge?' inquired Sara suspiciously.

'Don't know. Just wouldn't move so well, like it was rubbing on something. It was probably a bit of sticky snow or something. It goes great now. Watch this.' At that, he put his foot on it and kicked it towards the Idiots. They were speechless and stood there gaping at Bold and the sledge, which was now parked beside them.

How could it be? He must have got another sledge between here and the top. This one can't be it. It was smashed beyond repair.

There was no way they could work it out.

There was no point in them even trying to search for an answer as they would never in a million years come to the right conclusion. Smashed plastic sledges don't repair themselves. They just don't.

The Idiots left the other three and headed back into the town. There was silence all the way; they didn't speak to each other or suggest to each other possible explanations. They didn't want to be laughed at by the other. So they kept their crazy, weird explanations to themselves. And that was that. The end.

Of course, Amra and Sara had no idea of what had happened at the top. Sara, however, felt a bit uneasy; she suspected something had happened to Bold and had possibly involved the Idiots. His explanation about having 'sledge problems' was total nonsense. That much was obvious, but she had no idea what had happened, if anything at all, so she just let it be. If something had happened, she would find out sooner or later.

So Bold, Amra and Sara headed home. Bold with his miraculously repaired sledge, Sara with her unending curiosity and Amra with his incredible ability to be oblivious to the obvious. And Bold hoped tomorrow, eventually, would be a normal day.

Chapter 5 – A Very Cool Game of Basketball

Bold woke the next morning, later than his brother and sister. It was Sunday morning. He got up, opened the curtains and looked out of the living room window. It was much warmer today already. The snow was beginning to melt and the hills around the town were already a patchwork of brown and white.

The house was quiet. His mother had gone out for some groceries. Zolboo and Sara, he assumed, were sleeping in the bed in the backroom. Bold preferred sleeping on the floor in the living room, largely because he could watch Cartoon Network first thing in the morning or last thing at night when everybody else was all sleeping. He went through to the backroom. Nobody there!! Today was different indeed. He was the last person go get up and the house was more than quiet; it was empty. The weirdness of the last few days had taken its toll as he had slept a really long time. In fact, it was 11:15 in the morning and he can't remember ever having slept so long. Anyway, what was he going to do? Easy choice. Cartoon Network and then later in the afternoon have some breakfast.

So that was him until about 3 o'clock when his Mum and Zolboo returned after shopping and visiting his aunt who lived across the other side of town. She was obviously frustrated with Bold, bordering on angry.

'Bold. You been watching that all day?' she asked, waving loosely over towards the TV. He didn't hear her – too interested in 'Sid Mental and his dog Bark.' She switched the TV off and told him, 'Get yourself outside. It's a nice day again. Snow's melting.'

'Ok Mum,' he agreed. Three hours of cartoons were beginning to numb his brain. 'Can I take my basketball?' he asked.

'Sure.'

He went out to the balcony and searched around for his basketball. He hadn't seen it all winter.

'There it is.' It was lying over beside the stove. He picked it up and kicked some other stuff out the way. He brushed the snow and dirt off and took it inside.

'Found it,' he told his mum, who was putting Zolboo to sleep.

'Ok. Don't go far and be back around six.'

'Fine Mum,' he said, pushing his feet into his tied training shoes.

'And take your jacket.'

'Ok,' he said, grabbing it off the coat hook.

Two blocks away, there was a better court than the one outside his apartment. Kids tended to go there so he automatically headed in that direction. But then he stopped for a minute and thought through the logic. If he goes over there, there will be loads of kids already with a ball and he might not be able to play with his. Or maybe he won't be able to join in at all or if he does he will have to look out for his ball in case somebody pinches it.

'That's it. I'll stay here and play. Some kids will come over when they see I have a ball,' he said, trying to explain his reasoning to some invisible spectator.

So there he was, bouncing and practicing shooting on his own. As he had predicted earlier, it wasn't long before kids started coming over and within 30 minutes or so there was a full crowd of kids, girls and boys, all playing basketball or just hanging around.

Then Bold smiled to himself as he looked at his watch – 1630- and nothing weird had happened. Great. That was soon to change however.

Around five o'clock, kids began drifting off home or to somewhere else and half an hour later Bold was back on his own. He realized he needed to go home shortly but thought he'd hang on to the last minute. He had been playing well, scored many hoops and was pretty hyped-up and excited, so he began to show off a little to his invisible audience while giving a running TV commentary on his performance.

Shoot – straight in the hoop. He turned and shot in the other direction from half-way. Scored – no problem. He started bouncing and dribbling: crossover dribbles, between the legs, behind the back, wraparounds. He was doing them all but then he gradually began to notice he was putting less and less effort into actually bouncing the ball. But the ball was getting slightly higher with each bounce.....!

Bounce!   The height of the basketball stand.

Bounce!   Half way up the poplar tree beside the court.

Bounce!   Fourth storey apartment window.

Bounce!   *What's going on?* he thought. Higher than the 5 storey apartment building.

Bounce!   Higher again.

Bounce!   Higher again.

Then one last almighty bounce and all was silent. Where had the ball gone? Into space? And that is exactly where Bold was looking, head bent towards the stars, when he heard someone behind him.

'What you looking at nuthead?' said Dorj.

'Ehhh!' Bold turned round snapping out of his trance.

'What are you doing?' he repeated.

'Ehhh....Playing basketball. Ehhhh....what's it look like?'

Dorj looked around.

'Where's your ball? There's no ball here. You're mental. Gazing into space looking for spacemen or something no doubt.' No reply, just a silent pause.

'Apple juice! And now playing basketball with an invisible ball. Weirdo. And what happened to your sledge? I went up this morning to look for it.... And where did you get that new one. You are just weird.'

Bold looked up to the sky again, obviously not paying attention to his tormentors, just waiting to see if his ball would return.

'Stand over there. You defend that loop. This one is mine,' indicating the basketball stand next to him.

'Are you listening to me Nutter? Did you hear anything I just said?'

'Yes.' Pause. 'So stand over there and watch that hoop. I'm going to score. You have no chance.'

'You're a mental,' said Baatar, joining Dorj in his mocking of Bold. But Dorj obliged and went and guarded the loop anyway. More for entertainment value than actually believing this complete loony. He turned to Baatar and simply shrugged his shoulders.

'Wait! Get ready' advised Bold as he looked upwards. Dorj was beginning to worry a little now. *What was this loony doing?*

Bold was concentrating so hard and was so intense that Dorj was soon dragged into this impossibly silly situation as if it was a normal event – waiting for a ball to drop from the sky. Bold's intensity was so infectious it wasn't long before Dorj too, was bending his head upwards in anticipation for something, to happen, but he wasn't really sure what that would be.

Suddenly Bold saw a speck in the sky which quickly became a golf ball. Quicker. Closer. A tennis ball.........a football.

They both saw it and both began shaking and sweating profusely as this rocket ball came bulleting down towards them and suddenly....

'Ahhhh....' they both shouted, eyes popping out, mouths wide open. Fear and excitement and disbelief and adrenalin and more fear as the ball crashed through the hoop, scoring a miraculous point for Bold, before smashing into the ground, bouncing ferociously and careering skywards again. All in the blink of an eye.

Bold broke out of his ecstatic trance for a second as he heard Dorj and Baatar panicking and grabbing their coats off the ground and running away faster than they had ever ran before....

'...Ahhh!' they continued to cry, as they ran catapulting over the broken park benches and see-saws. They looked back in terror at Bold who was still fixated to the sky. *Will the ball ever come back?* He thought to himself. Oh yes, and he didn't have long to wait.

The ball came crashing down towards the hoop, but this time it didn't go through it, as Bold was expecting. In fact, it seemed to be slowing down the closer it got to the basketball court. Closer and closer. Slower and slower. Then Bold managed to grab hold of it with both his hands. He immediately let one hand go as if he was going to bounce it again. So he bounced it and the ball came back up almost instantly.

Bold got ready for another bounce and almost instantly the ball smashed off the ground and catapulted back up to Bold. But when his hand made contact with the ball, it stuck solid. And before he realized what was happening, he was heading skywards. He didn't know what was happening until he sensed his hand was stuck fast to the ball.

Everything was a complete blur – all he could do was yell 'Ahhhhh...' He didn't know whether he was upside down or the right way round or how fast he was going, or if he was going upwards, downwards, sideways, backwards or forwards.

Down below, a few stray dogs witnessed this event and started barking towards the sky, hair standing up on their backs. One however, thought it better to scamper away as quickly as possible, tail between its hind legs. A few people witnessed these strange behaving dogs but could never have guessed as to what was really going on.

Meanwhile, high above, a 10 year old boy was whirling around the sky, hands stuck fast to a basketball that thought it was a jet fighter plane.

'Ahhhhh.......' heard the dogs and a few imaginative or alert humans far down below (who probably reckoned somebody was shouting from one of the apartment blocks).

Again, the ball and Bold came crashing towards the ground but this time, Bold was beginning to lose his fear. His hand was stuck tight to the ball and he sensed it would be impossible to break loose. He started cautiously to look down at the familiar places he knew – the football stadium, the power station, the lake, the basketball court...

eh.. THE BASKETBALL COURT??

.....CRASH......

He wasn't paying attention as the ball bounced off the court again and rocketed up towards the sky, Bold still attached and incredibly, undamaged. And so it went on for maybe half an hour or more. Up, down, back and forth, Bold enjoying every minute of this crazy and magical ride in the sky.

Back on land, the dogs still sat attentively in a row and, ears up and heads cocked sideways, watched the aerial display until the ball and Bold disappeared over the skyline and landed slowly and safely on some piece of vacant grassland out of sight of any prying eyes (dog or human).

Exhausted, Bold lay on the ground and was soon fast asleep. An hour later, the dogs found him and started licking his face to wake him up, which he did. He then slowly got to his feet, his legs and arms being rather sore, looked around to see where he was and if his basketball was here (it wasn't).

He then headed straight home. On arriving home he went straight out to the balcony. Sure enough, his basketball was there, leaning against the stove. Bold never noticed that the blue light was still on.

Chapter 6 - Exercise Time

The weekend was over. Back to school on Monday. Bold generally liked school and was good at most of his subjects but today was his favourite day, sports day, and he was excited. He got up early, did what he had to do – get dressed, have breakfast, brush teeth – only this morning, much quicker and with much more enthusiasm than normal. Sports day lay ahead.

On arriving at school, he found most of his classmates had got there sooner and had begun getting changed into their sports clothes. First event was the wrestling. Bold didn't care for this much. There were bigger and stronger boys in the school so he wasn't bothered too much when the wrestling was finished.

Next was the long jump. Again, he wasn't too bothered about letting that pass. Then it was the running and that is what Bold really liked. He was fast, fit and had longer legs than most of the others; this is what he assumed gave him an advantage. His classmates knew he was one of the fastest boys, but they also knew he was also one of the best at running distances. So, first the sprinting and, as expected, Bold did well and came second only to Dash, who was a sporting genius as well as having a rather appropriate name for a boy who could run fast.

The last event was the one Bold had been waiting for; the run up the hill behind the school. He was expected to win this. It was only a few kilometers up to the top and back but the track was, in parts, both muddy and dusty and the top of the hill was very stony, so runners had to be very careful as not to fall. Once at the top, they had to run around the stone cairn three times and return back down the hill.

'Ready. Go,' said Mr. Bagi the sports teacher. And they were off. Bold dashed off to the front almost immediately and hardly looked back the whole race. He felt good and wasn't tiring too much until he got to the stony summit which was always more difficult. The cairn was closing fast and soon he was running around it. Once. Twice. Three times and finished. Now back down to the school.

(He didn't realize this at the time, but on his first lap around the cairn a small stone lodged itself into the sole of one of his training shoes).

He arrived back at school first with most of the other children all scattered around or drawn-out behind him almost all the way up to the top of the hill. He felt good that he had come first, however, he was very, very thirsty so he gulped down a bottle of water and started his celebrations.

An hour later, he was standing outside the door of his apartment knocking. Sara had the day-off college and was working on her project. She opened the door but just grunted.

'I won the race up the hill. It was easy. Gold medal,' he said trying in vain to impress his sister.

'Great,' she replied, obviously not in the slightest bit interested.

'Any food?' he asked 'I'm starving,' he continued as he was taking his shoes off. He was still pumping with adrenalin, even though he had dozed off on the grass at the school for a few minutes, before being woken by Mr. Bagi.

'There is some new bread and instant noodles and some soup from yesterday.' He went into the kitchen to investigate, carrying his dusty and dirty shoes with him.

'Oh. Tomato and Strawberry soup,' he said as he stared into the big pot of soup on the cooker. Tomato and Strawberry soup was his favourite.

'........And clean your shoes AND the floor before mum comes back and sees your mess.' He thought his sister must be psychic. How did she know he had made a mess? But she was right. It was best to clean up before thinking about food.

But he would sweep the floor first and then do his shoes later after his stomach had been taken care of. So he opened the balcony door, tossed his shoes casually over there somewhere and went back in to eat some lunch. The shoes landed haphazardly, one on the balcony floor, one in a plastic bucket, which was sitting on the stove and which then toppled over, sending the shoe downwards to the floor.

On the way down the small stone imbedded in one of the shoes, bashed against the blue light.

The stone didn't come loose, however. In fact, all the bashing and bumping imbedded the stone even further into the shoe. The blue light didn't come on. Not yet. But it would latter.

Bold gobbled down the food and had completely forgotten about the weirdness of the last few days. In fact, nothing weird happened that day (apart from his sister actually cleaning up the kitchen after he had already done it – he thought that was pretty weird!). It was a normal day. Back to normal. Tomorrow, however, would certainly not be.

That night everyone slept soundly. It was a calm night. No wind. No Dust.

But at around 0315 the light came on.

The next morning Bold got up as normal. His mother had already left to go to work early, Sara was in the kitchen making breakfast and young Zolboo was still at his Grandmothers. Everything was normal. So Bold went to school, done his work and played with his friends at break-time.

The morning flew past and soon it was time to go home. At twelve o'clock the kids ate their lunch and headed home. Bold was in the school car park when it all started.

'Throw it here,' shouted one boy, who caught the ball and threw it at Bold.

'Missed,' Bold shouted, arching his back and seeing the ball bounce away down the slope. Another boy ran down and collected it. He kicked it high up in the air. The other boys were looking up and waiting for it. Big scramble as the kids bashed into each other, each trying to grab the ball as it landed. Bold got there first but came crashing down on the ground, not letting go. The other kids tried to wrestle it from his hands, all unsuccessfully, all laughing together at the same time. Bold eventually managed to wriggle free from the entangled mass of boys and stand up. They would have to try harder to get the ball back from him. He looked around briefly for somewhere to escape to. The cars! He started running over to the group of cars parked in the car park. The others followed, some of them beginning to get irritated at Bold's unsporting behavior. Bold ran around one car, then another, some kids following, some kids trying to block him off. Eventually they started getting tired or bored with the chasing game and drifted off.

'Let's go and play at the park,' one boy said.

'I'm going to the shop to get some juice,' said another.

Bold continued to keep running around the same car. Not too fast, but not simply jogging either. In fact, he wanted to stop but somehow his legs kept going. Kept running and running. Not getting faster and not getting slower but he kept going around and around the car. Soon he was alone, as all the kids had gone and it was just him left and the cars. And his legs - running and running.

Why I am not getting tired? He thought to himself.

'Why are you running around that car?' asked a little boy who had suddenly just appeared.

'I don't know,' he answered truthfully 'I'm practicing for a competition,' he continued, trying to justify his strange behavior.

'Better hurry up then. You're not very fast.'

At home, the light on the stove slowly started to shine

Soon another boy appeared and the first boy told him that the runner was practicing for a competition. Olympics I think it was.

'Do you think you will win?' he asked.

No answer. The boys just stood and watched the lone runner running round and round the car. One hour past, then two but by then the two boys were long gone and another group of passers-by had begun arriving. First an old woman came, then a bunch of students, then some businessmen going home from work. It wasn't long before about 50 people were standing around Bold watching him run around the car all asking the same questions and getting the same reply. Things were definitely getting weird.

Eventually the owner of the car, a teacher named Mr. Erdene, came out. He wanted to go home and as such he shouted at Bold —

'Hey Bold. What are you doing? I need to go home now. You need to stop running around my car. I need to go home now.'

'I can't. I would like to stop but, honestly sir, I can't.'

The audience around the car was rather puzzled at this.

'What do you mean you can't?' someone asked.

'I can't. I just can't.'

It was true. Bold was no longer in control of his legs. He wasn't getting tired but also couldn't speed up. It was as if he was on Auto-pilot or had Cruise control switched on in a car. Mr. Erdene was getting more than irritated now. But he was also beginning to sense that the crowd wouldn't let him get in his car — they were mesmerized by this running boy and, if Mr. Erdene was honest with himself, he was getting to be like that also. There was something happening here that nobody could understand; and nobody could really understand why they were all so enchanted by this boy, this boy who was running round a car and who had been so for the last four hours without a stop.

Back at home, the light on the stove was now shining brightly.

As Bold kept running, the stone in his shoe became almost completely imbedded in the sole. There was no escape.

One more hour passed, then two. Then the local newspaper people came and shortly after the TV people, not to mention the police, all of his teachers and even some people from some local companies who thought they could cash in on the events –

'Bold, the incredible running boy, uses Adidas sneakers – now available at Batar's Sporting Bazar.'

Then suddenly without warning Bold stopped; he stumbled forward for a few paces as if somebody had gently pushed him, but he had stopped running. People, strangely enough, seemed disappointed, not to say curious, as to why he stopped.

'Why did you stop?' said one.

'What are you doing?' said another.

'Tired?' One old man asked.

'I don't know. I'm not tired,' Bold was as puzzled as his audience, who all started chatting to each other trying to discover if they had missed something. Bold had been running for 6 hours and didn't feel at all tired or even thirsty. The crowd put it down to his long distance running ability, which they had all become aware of due to his sports day victory from the previous morning. Bold couldn't explain it but knew inside something weird had happened again. This time though, it was not as obvious as weird taps, a sledge repairing itself in front of his eyes or flying around the sky holding onto a basketball. It was more subtle, more delicate. He never did realize that it was because the stone in his shoe which he picked up when running three times around the cairn had eventually come loose and fallen out. And, of course, linking any of the strange events to the old stove sitting on his balcony would be completely out of the question.

Chapter 7 - Decision Time

The old man knew he didn't have much time left. He had had a good life but now he knew he had to make preparations for the future. Not his future but the future of the stove. He knew who would be able to look after it, who would be able to make best use out of it and who, more practically, would be able to 'find' it.

He didn't live in the Gobi anymore and had moved to the town. He still lived in his yurt but on the outskirts of town, alone in his yurt but with some good friends and relatives close by. He was content with life. He put his bowl of milky tea on top of his shiny new stove and stood up, making his way towards the door. Outside was getting cold but the old man liked that. He went over to the old shack in the corner and stood for a while looking into it, looking at his old stove that had given him so much adventure (and trouble!) in the past. He thought out loud to himself -

'Those were good times, but I'm too old now. It's time for you to move on,' speaking both to himself and the stove. It was time to pass the stove on to the next person. A man from another yurt nearby came over and offered to help take the stove away.

They loaded the disassembled parts onto the back of the truck.

'Thanks,' he said to the young guy in his 20's. However, he told the young guy he had to do the next part himself. He had to put the stove in a place where the next person would find it, somebody who would, for whatever reason, want to have the stove, somebody with a sense of adventure, somebody who was curious and bright and interested in everything around him — someone who always asked 'why' and 'how' and never just accepted things. He remembered Bold from when they both lived in the desert. He had taken an interest in the young boy ever since and knew he would be the perfect person to take possession of the stove. But he couldn't just give it to him. Bold would have to find it and take it home, to show he was adventurous enough. To show he had *The Right Stuff*.

The old man drove slowly but soon enough he arrived at the drainage ditch. In a few days it would be getting cleaned out, but right now it was filthy. He didn't mind, he knew what he had to do. He saw the tunnel under the road up ahead and parked as close as he could to the entrance. He took up his little bag of tools from beneath the passenger seat and went round to the back of his old pick-up and started to take the parts of the stove off the back. One by one he took them down into the tunnel until all the parts were accounted for. He switched on his torch and started to assemble the stove. Once he had finished, he half covered it in whatever was lying around. It had not to be too easy to see, nor too difficult to find. When he was satisfied, he put his tools away and headed out to the truck again.

'*That should do it,*' he thought out loud to himself as he hauled himself up the bank of the ditch.

Chapter 8 - Communication Problems

Sports day was over and today would be a normal school day. Tuesday would be like any other Tuesday – Math's first, then some Mongolian Language and then some.....English. That's right. Bold had nearly forgotten they were starting English lessons today. A woman had come from abroad to teach them English and they were going to start today just after lunch, I think.

The secondary school next door had an English teacher last year but he had gone home and some other teacher from some other country had taken his place and was teaching them some other language – Japanese or Korean, he couldn't remember which. That's right! It was Korean, the language all the soap operas on the TV use before they get overdubbed. In fact, everybody was a bit obsessed with Korea - the Korean pop music stars, the film actors and actresses. Even Kimchi, that spicy cabbage which Bold hated but some people in his family, notably his sister, could actually eat.

'Yuk,' Bold said out loud as he entered school, picturing his sister eating those horrible bits of red spicy cabbage, 'I'm never going to eat that.'

'What did you say?' said a boy pushing past Bold. The boy looked at his friend and shrugged. Bold ignored them both and continued along the corridor to his classroom, still imagining his sister with the Kimchi.

The previous night had been another calm and peaceful night. Everything had been quiet on the balcony. Inside Sara had just finished her spicy Korean Kimchi noodles and Bold was complaining to her about the smell.

'How can you eat that?' he had complained to his sister, 'it is horrible.'

At that, he had gone over to the kitchen table and had grabbed the empty tub of Dong Shin noodles, taken it over to the window, opened the top window and tossed the tub onto the balcony.

'Blahhh..' he had complained to his sister, screwing his face up.

'Eh! I hadn't finished eating that,' she had protested, knowing full well that it was empty.

'It IS empty,' he had pointed out, 'anyway, you'll stink the kitchen out eating that.'

Sara had wanted to slap him or kick his bum,

but reckoned that would have caused more trouble than it was worth. So she had resorted to typical teenage angst, 'God, you are so annoying. Why don't you just grow up,' she had ranted as she stormed out the kitchen. Bold did what he usually did and ignored her.

Outside on the balcony, it was still quiet. The only difference was that there was a small blue light glowing from the stove. The empty Kimchi tub had hit the stove on the way down to the balcony floor.

Bold entered the classroom and sat down at his desk and took out his pencil and notebook from his bag. The first class was Mongolian Language, which was a bit tedious but bearable. The class was still noisy as the teacher shuffled about today's lesson's teaching material. Bold was strangely quiet. He was in a bit of a bad mood – or so it seemed. He couldn't be bothered with his classmates today and kept himself to himself.

'Ok kids, settle down,' said the teacher again. 'Do you have your homework Bold?' Bold muttered something under his breath.

'What was that?' the teacher pounced back, not understanding what Bold had said.

Bold replied. This time the teacher heard and so did many of his classmates. This time they gradually stopped whatever they were doing and turned to Bold, who was a little unnerved by the sudden increase in the attention he was getting.

'What are you saying? This is Mongolian class. What language are you speaking Bold,' she half demanded as she continued to flip through her class materials. Bold thought she was behaving strangely and screwed his face up at this weird response from his teacher'

'Eh.......Mongolian?' he replied thinking he was making a really funny joke at his teachers expense and expecting some reward from his classmates for doing so. The attention did increase, but not in the way he expected. Now all eyes were on him and some jaws had even fallen to the floor. To Bold, of course and to Bold's EARs, he had spoken Mongolian – he couldn't speak any other languages, just a few words he had picked up from TV and elsewhere.

But for everyone else, they didn't hear

Mongolian, because to them, and their ears, he was speaking Korean. Yip, that's right. Korean.

'What are you all looking at?' he demanded (in Mongolian) of his classmates (who heard Korean).

Silence with some secretive whispers and nervous laughing.

'What language is that?' 'Can he speak Chinese?' 'What's he doing?' 'Is he mad?' More whispers, shuffling, nervous laughing.

'Bold!!!' demanded his teacher, obviously getting angrier.

'You must stop that at once, it is not being funny or smart. You must stop right now and start speaking Mongolian. If you don't' you will be in big trouble.'

Bold was completely dumbstruck.

'I am speaking Mongolian,' he insisted, 'I am speaking Mongolian. Are you.....?' He slowly stopped and looked around rather cautiously, at the same time sinking into his chair. Everybody was staring at him. Nobody understood anything he was saying.

'What are you all looking at me for?' he said, rather more timidly. Nobody understood of course. 'What's wrong with you all?' Nobody understood of course. He was speaking Korean. Then it struck him like lightning. The 'weirdness' had returned. Something was wrong and he didn't know exactly what, but nobody understood him. So he decided to be quiet and speak as little as possible to see if whatever was wrong would somehow disappear and normality would return. Deep down, he suspected it might not be that simple.

His teacher stared at Bold wondering what the next step was. She decided to ignore him. He was wanting attention, she decided. And he wasn't going to get it. So for the rest of the class Bold didn't speak and nobody spoke to Bold.

At the end of class, the children were dismissed as normal but Bold was ordered to stay behind and explain his behaviour which, of course, he did. In Korean. On hearing him continuing to speak in Korean and refusing to speak in Mongolian, his teacher, Mrs Bileg, demanded of him one last time to speak in Mongolian.

'I know you are speaking Korean,' she said, 'I don't know where you learnt it and it is impressive that you can. But...,' she paused, 'you are not allowed to speak it in this class. So stop playing the fool and speak to me in your native tongue,' she waited for his reply. 'Instantly,' she added for extra strength. He knew he had to reply and he hoped, prayed, begged that this time he would be understood. Had the waiting game worked? Well, here goes. He took a big, deep breath and paused. Paused again. And then again, just in case. *OK, this time, ready - here goes......*

'I am speaking Mongolian,' he said, hoping he was, indeed, speaking Mongolian. But no. It was still Korean. On hearing this, his teacher paused, thought and suddenly walked rather quickly, kind of comically thought Bold, out the classroom. Then she came straight back

'Right! And YOU stay here. Do not leave this room,' she made that very clear, as she again stormed off, this time to the secondary school next door in search of Kim Young Su, the young Korean teacher who was working at the school.

Five minutes later she returned with Mr. Kim, who was a little puzzled as to what was going on.

'Bold is not speaking Mongolian and everything he says is in Korean,' she told him, 'we can't understand him and he is refusing to co-operate with us. Can you tell him to stop speaking Korean and start speaking Mongolian? Please.'

'Ok,' he said in Korean, as he turned to Bold. 'Hi Bold, my name is Kim Young Su. I am Korean and I teach at the secondary school next door. Your teacher says you can speak Korean but she wants you to speak Mongolian now. She is impressed with your language skills but you need to start speaking Mongolian. She is very angry.'

'I don't understand all this. I AM speaking Mongolian but nobody understands me. I AM speaking Mongolian. I hear Mongolian when I speak, but everybody thinks I'm speaking some other language.' Eh! So Mr. Kim was speaking Korean but this time Bold was hearing Mongolian – so Bold understood. Bizarre.

'That is very funny Bold. But you do not need to joke anymore,' Mr. Kim paused and then smiled, 'however, I am sure everyone will be happy now.' Mr. Kim, who had studied Mongolian, was relieved that Bold was now speaking Mongolian again and he didn't really understand what all the fuss was.

74

Wait a minute! Mongolian? Well, Bold WAS speaking Mongolian and Mr. Kim WAS also hearing Mongolian. But, how was he to know that everybody else in the room had just heard Bold and Mr. Kim's conversation in Korean..........?

Satisfied he had been of help and had solved the problem, he turned to Bold's teacher and said (a little smugly), 'he seems fine now. He says he can't speak Korean and only knows Mongolian. May I go now? I have a class shortly.'

Bold's teacher could not believe what she had just heard and Bold's classmates gasped in disbelief as they looked at each other. *Is that really what Bold and Mr. Kim had said?* Mr. Kim and Bold while trying to figure out what had just happened and why everybody was behaving as strangely as they were.

Everybody in the class had just heard Mr. Kim and Bold speaking Korean together. They didn't understand, of course, but they knew it wasn't Mongolian. If that wasn't strange enough, then Mr. Kim had turned around and, in Mongolian, told everybody, Mrs. Bileg and the whole class, that Bold couldn't speak Korean or indeed any other foreign language!

What was he talking about? What was he playing at? Everybody just had just heard them both speak Korean. Mr. Kim's helpful and satisfied mood came to an abrupt end.

'I don't know what you two are up to here,' she scowled at Mr. Kim and Bold, 'but I am not an idiot and I will not be made a fool of by anybody. Mr. Kim, I will be informing your supervisor of your rude and disrespectful behaviour'.

Mr Kim and Bold looked at each other in complete disbelief. *Has everybody gone mad?* They thought.

'Told you so,' Bold said. 'Everybody thinks I am speaking Korean. What language am I speaking now?' he asked Mr. Kim (in Mongolian).

'Mongolian,' Mr. Kim replied. Then a pause.

'Naturally,' he added, seemingly confused.

'What language was I speaking earlier?'

'Same. Mongolian.' Mr. Kim was completely baffled by all this. He was also upset as to what Bold's teacher had just told him. He was also worried about his supervisor being contacted. What was he going to do? He had one more class that day. He thought he had better go back to his apartment for a rest before he could face another class. At that, he turned away from Bold and quietly headed out the door.

'I need to go home now,' he said to Bold as he went, 'Bye.'

'See you tomorrow Mr. Kim,' Bold replied, being rather unsure that he actually would.

They were speaking Mongolian of course. The strange thing was that the other kids around them heard them speak also – and this time, they too, heard Mongolian. Their Korean had disappeared. Now everybody was back to speaking and HEARING Mongolian. And everything was back to normal. The weirdness had finished for the day. Bold noticed all this and smiled happily. Mr. Kim, of course, didn't – he had no idea about any of the strange things that had happened to Bold over the last few days. Bold and some of the other kids started playing around and talking, laughing and shouting again - In Mongolian, of course. Mr. Kim, however, remained rather confused over the whole event for a much longer time...

'Maybe this time,' Bold thought out loud, 'Maybe this time, everything will be back to normal.'

'Pleeeaaasse....' he added as an after note. He looked up as if he was asking some higher power above, 'No more weirdness,' he pleaded to whoever up there was listening.

Back at Bold's house, his sister had just left. She was carrying three plastic bags of trash including the empty noodle cartons that had been lying around on the balcony. She went over to the large pile of plastic, moldy food, old bottles and empty packaging that passed as a make-do waste collection point and threw the bags on top of the rotting heap. The crows, the dogs and their scraggly puppies lunged in to see what goodies had been delivered. The Kimchi had gone. And the light on the stove was out.

Chapter 9 – The Return of the Old Man

The old man sat on the broken park bench. He was content as he watched the kids playing basketball on the old court. The grass around him was beginning to grow again and push up through the melting snow and broken glass strewn all over the ground. He had made his decision. He would meet Bold.

Soon enough, Bold appeared around the corner carrying his school stuff and talking with a couple of friends. The old man watched him, completely at ease with the world around him. He came closer, closer to the basketball court that had been the scene of his magical flying episode a few days before. Already by now Bold was beginning to think he had imagined the whole thing. He saw the old man out the corner of his eyes but didn't recognize him or pay much attention to him either. Then suddenly the old man ushered him to come over a little closer. Bold looked at his friend and shrugged. Maybe the old man needed something from the shop.

'Hello,' said the old man, 'how are you today?'

'Fine,' Bold said, frowning at the same time. It

seemed a rather strange question. Then the old man waited.

'You don't know who I am, do you?' The boy seemed a little disinterested.

'I am your uncle. You used to visit me years ago when we both lived in the South Gobi.' Now, *that* got Bold's attention.

'What?'

'I am your uncle Bayar.' There was a pause.

'Can I ask you a question, my boy?' the old man inquired.

'Eh....ok. Sure.'

'Has anything...hmmm....strange or unusual happened to you recently? I mean not normal. Definitely unusual.'

Bold didn't say anything. He just stood and stared at the old man, intrigued as to what the old man was saying, who he really was and where he had really come from.

'All these strange things that have been happening to you. You know what I mean. They happened to me also when I was a boy. Have you thought about why they are happening? Or how they are happening?' He asked rhetorically or half expecting an answer.

'Well, I know.' That last sentence started the adrenalin racing in Bold's heart. *How did this old man know these things?*

'I will tell you the secret. I will SHOW you the secret. Now go home and ask your mother if you can come over to your Uncle Bayar's yurt. She knows where I live but she hasn't visited in many years. Too busy I suppose. Come on Saturday, in the afternoon. Come alone. Your mother has my phone number, or maybe *had*, but you could give me hers also, just in case she hasn't,' he gestured towards boy.

'Ok, it is 95768543.'

'I will phone her later.' He paused and considered the lie he had just told as he had no intention of phoning. 'Anyway, I better get going. I need to light the stove,' he said without a hint of irony.

'See you on Saturday,' said Bold hesitantly as the old man got up and headed along the rough

82

path towards the shop.

'Uncle Bayar?' he said to himself, 'I think I can vaguely remember him.'

'Oh and my yurt....' said the old man turning back towards Bold and as if he had forgotten to mention it '...is the last one before the forest a few kilometers out of town. Get off at the last bus-stop and I'll be there waiting.'

Bold didn't reply but he thought it strange as none of them had mentioned what time they were to meet. Anyway, Bold just figured that old men knew all that kind of stuff, times and meetings and arrangements and all that.

Saturday came without any further weird incidents. Everything was back to normal again. Bold's mum went to work and his sister took his baby brother out to get some new summer clothes. Bold didn't tell his mum about his plans to go to his uncle's yurt. She would never allow Bold to go on his own, so he simply didn't mention it. He would get a bus to the end of town and then just walk the rest. He arrived at the bus stop at about lunchtime and was surprised to see the Old Man waiting for him.

'How are you, Bold?' he inquired.

'Fine. Where is your yurt?' Bold was anxious to find out more about whatever the Old Man knew.

'Not far. So what have been doing this week?' The old man asked as they headed along the road towards Uncle Bayar's yurt. It was obvious Bold and his Uncle Bayar would get along just fine. So they chatted until they arrived at Uncle Bayar's yurt. The hours went past. They laughed and played together in the yurt and also outside. The Old Man also showed all the old photographs that he had kept. Bold, as always, was as curious as ever.

'What's this one? Who are these people? What is this thing for?'

His curiosity seemed endless. He wanted to know everything.

Then suddenly Bold stopped. Some photo had caught the side of his eye. He peered down, sweeping gently some other photos aside.

Right there in front of him was a photo he could hardly believe he was seeing. A boy, around ten. Standing beside.... a stove. He looked closer. Yes, it was. It was HIS stove. The one he hauled back to his house a week ago. How did his Uncle Bayar have it? *No. All stoves look the same,* he thought. But no. This one did look different.

'I know,' his Uncle said, 'you are correct. That is the stove you now have on your balcony. The very same one I (ahem)...*happened across...* all these years ago.' Then he said something that both scared and excited Bold and answered about every question he had asked himself the last few days.....

'..and gave me all the impossible adventures that a ten year boy could only dream of in an entire lifetime.'

Bold was now completely mesmerized by the photo, while asking himself about a thousand questions all at the same time, each one as unanswerable and confusing as the previous and next.

'Many years ago when I was your age, an old man, like myself, gave me it. He told me he had made it himself from metal....and some strange blue glass he had found way out in the desert. He never really explained exactly what or where but it was like some sort of metal junkyard with scrap metal and bits of old burnt stuff lying everywhere. There was a lot of this blue glass he told me. But he could only collect a little of it and he had already lost some when he met me. He said it shined and he liked the effect of the shining so he built it into a stove he was making... as a sort of decoration I suppose. Shining blue lights.'

'Shining blue lights?' Bold was baffled. Of course, he had never seen the blue lights, although he had certainly experienced their effects.

Uncle Bayar then suggested that they just wait to see if anything happened. Bold was a bit confused but was still intrigued by all the old photos, so they waited. But nothing happened. 5 minutes. 10 minutes. Bold was getting a little bored now. Nothing was going to happen.

'Let's do something else, let's go outside,' Bold said.

'Ok. A few more minutes,' replied his Uncle, who then seemed to have another idea, 'I have something else.' Uncle Bayar got up from his stool and pulled out a little orange box from beneath his bed. 'I have some spare blue glass pieces. They were given to me by the man who built the stove. He said they were 'spares' but I never needed to replace anything. I always thought it was a bit strange really. So I just put them in the box. I take them out and show them to people on special occasions.'

He then emptied them on to the top of the stove and moved them around a little. Then shuffled them a bit more.

'Why are you doing that?' asked Bold.

'Just trying something out,' said his uncle, 'do you know something? I am glad you found the stove. Maybe these pieces do have a purpose after all. Let's just wait and watch, shall we.'

They waited. And waited but nothing seemed to happen. Bold didn't really know what to expect, but after the last few days, anything was possible. Then something happened. Some shards of glass suddenly moved very slowly along the top of the stove. Very slowly, but definitely moving.

Bold gasped, put his hands to his mouth and tried not to say or do anything. Then a sudden jerk, very soft but definite. Then the floor began to move, ever so slightly.

Bold looked a little scared, 'What was that?' he asked, a little panic in his voice.

'I don't know.'

Then, suddenly, the floor very slowly started rotating. Just a crawling pace, barely moving at all. Then not just the floor, but it seemed the whole yurt was beginning to rotate, everything apart from the stove and chimney in the middle, which remained static. Things gently started to rattle and clang; the cutlery and jars, the plates and pots. Very gently but gradually getting noisier as the yurt speeded up.

Then the yurt darkened slightly as if somebody had dimmed the lights and the whole yurt became bathed in a very faint blue light. The spinning started to speed up, still nowhere near walking speed but moving nonetheless. Then Bold felt a butterfly in his stomach. He was sure the yurt was moving upwards.

'What is happening, Uncle Bayar?'

His Uncle smiled. He seemed at total ease with the weird happenings around him – unlike Bold who was desperate to know all the answers, right away. Any fear Bold originally had, was now replaced with awe and excitement.

'Wow. What is happening, Uncle Bayar?' he repeated as he tried to take in what was happening.

'I think we may be about to have....' he paused, '...a new great adventure. Perhaps the greatest one we will ever have.'

On the outskirts of the city, just out of sight of the last of the yurts, everything seemed peaceful, quiet and normal. Families bedded down for the night, lights flickered off, TVs went silent, babies stopped crying.

One yurt, however, was far from normal. This lone isolated yurt was hovering over the ground, slowly spinning while strange blue light shone out from the circular skylight in the centre and from between the raised, floating floor and the ground. The spinning got slowly faster, the yurt rose slowly higher. And....

And all stopped.... The lights went out.....The motion stopped...3 seconds standing still about 1 metre off the ground. All was silent and still again. Bold and Uncle Bayar froze, but they weren't scared. Not at all. Bold was smiling the biggest smile he had ever smiled and his uncle sat silently watching him.

Then something totally incredible and unexpected happened. The yurt shot up towards the sky, changed direction and vanished over the horizon.

Whoosh and it was gone.

But inside were an old man and a ten year old boy. Two special people who had the gift of curiosity. Two special people who were, as Uncle Bayar predicted, about to embark on the biggest adventure they would ever have.

Bold's next big adventure was, indeed, about to begin.

Bold – FACTFILE

Age – around 10, but it changes every year

<u>Favourite Stuff</u>

Food – strawberry and Tomato soup

Clothes – his red 'Tea-shirts'

Car – Ferramborghini 5 Billion

Sport – Batball

Girl! – Yuk...

Hobbies-fixing stuff and flying basketball

Place – outside

Drink – Bazooka-ade

Colour – red (of course)

Music- The Pajama Dinosaurs

Cartoon Character – Sid Mental and his dog Bark

Movie – eat my Brain 2 (the first one was rubbish)

Follow Bold on Facebook ☐ Bold Badrongan

30566347R00058

Printed in Poland
by Amazon Fulfillment
Poland Sp. z o.o., Wrocław